WARNING

Any relationship to any historical fact WHATSOEVER is entirely coincidental.

YOU HAVE BEEN WARNED

You don't HAVE to read the Hiccup books in order.
But if you want to, this is the right order:

1. How to train your Dragon
2. How to be a Pirate
3. How to speak Dragonese
4. How to Cheat a Dragon's Curse
5. How to Twist a Dragon's Tale
6. A Hero's Guide to Deadly Dragons
7. How to Ride a Dragon's Storm
8. How to Break a Dragon's Heart
9. How to Steal a Dragon's Sword

This book has been specially
written and published for
World Book Day 2012.

For further information please see
www.worldbookday.com

World Book Day in the UK and Ireland is made possible by generous
sponsorship from National Book Tokens, participating publishers, authors and
booksellers. Booksellers who accept the £1 World Book Day Token bear the
full cost of redeeming it.

HICCUP
and his
dragon. Toothless

ABOUT HICCUP

Hiccup Horrendous Haddock the Third was
an awesome swordfighter, a dragon-whisperer,
and the greatest Viking Hero that ever lived.
But Hiccup's memoirs look back to when
he was a very ordinary boy, and finding
it hard to be a Hero.

HICCUP
(the Hero of this story)

TOOTHLESS
(Hiccup's hunting dragon)

SNOTLOUT
(Hiccup's cousin)

FIREWORM
(really mean hunting dragon belonging to SNOTLOUT)

THE DREADER
(terrifying Seadragon keeping everyone hostage on Berk)

Gobber
the
Belch.
(Warrior in charge of the
Pirate Training Programme)

Fishlegs
(Hiccup's best
friend)

STOICK
the
VAST
(Hiccup's father
who is the Chief)

Mum

This book is dedicated to my grandpa ALAN and my grandmas Nancy and JILL because they all told me stories.

A Catalogue record for this book is available from the British Library

ISBN: 978 1 444 90773 5

Printed and bound by CPI Group (UK) Ltd, Croydon, CR0 4YY

The paper and board used in this paperback book by Hodder Children's Books are natural recyclable products made from wood grown in sustainable forests. The manufacturing processes conform to the environmental regulations of the country of origin.

Hodder Children's Books
a division of Hachette Children's Books
338 Euston Road, London NW1 3BH
An Hachette UK Company
www.hachette.co.uk

The Day of the Dreader

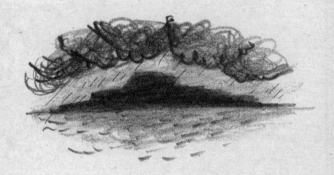

CRESSIDA COWELL

Hodder
Children's
Books

a division of Hachette Children's Books

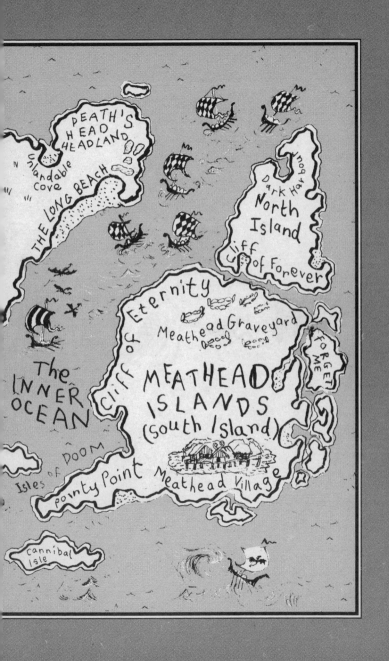

~ CONTENTS ~

absolutely, completely
and TOTALLY!

The True
Story of
the
Day of the
Dreader

Stories do not always tell the truth.
Except for this one.
Many stories have been told about
what happened on THE DAY OF THE

PROLOGUE

Stories do not always tell the truth…
Except for this one.

Many stories have been told about what happened on **THE DAY OF THE DREADER**. Many sagas have been sung by the bards at the fireside. But I have to warn you, dear reader or listener, stories do not always tell the truth. The bard gets carried away. Legends get added to and exaggerated, and so gradually, gradually… the truth gets lost along the way.

Here, for the very first time, I shall tell you the real story, the truth about what really happened on that dreadful day…

It *is* the truth, I promise.

One terrible winter, a truly dreadful Seadragon rose up from the depths of the ocean like a bad mood from Thor and swam to the waters surrounding the little Isle of Berk and took root in the dark mud there. You could not see him; all that was visible was a long dark shadow, a deep depression in the water that was so big it was almost as long as the island itself.

The name of that Seadragon was a 'Dreader'.

The Dreader was no ordinary Seadragon.

Every single dragon in the ocean was frightened of a Dreader.

Sharkworms and Darkbreathers and Doomfangs all scattered like flies at the sight of it. Even a much larger dragon like the mighty Seadragonus Giganticus Maximus, a dragon the size of an underwater mountain, would give a snort of terror when it spotted a Dreader on the horizon, and with one flap of its mighty tail, it would disappear into the depths of the ocean.

For it was said that a Dreader had a power that was truly dreadful indeed.

Legend had it that it sucked out every drop of moisture from its victim's

body, leaving it as thin and desiccated as a piece of paper. Or it merely removed its senses, or its brain or its heart, leaving it mad as a box of frogs, or a lifeless lump of flesh.

The Hooligans were so frightened of the Dreader lurking by their shore, that no boats or hunting-dragons could leave the island to hunt fish. They were waiting for the Dreader to go away.

They waited, and waited, and waited.

And as they waited, they ate everything they could find on the little Isle of Berk.

They ate all the fat black mussels that clung to the rocks. They ate all the scallops and oysters and big juicy clams they could find on the beaches.

But the Dreader would not go away.

And slowly but surely, the Hooligans and the dragons on the little Isle of Berk began to starve…

Slowly, but
Surely, the
Hooligans began
to STARVE.

Hiccup
Horrendous
HAddock →
the
THiRd.

1. THE CLEVER AND INTELLIGENT PLAN

Six weeks after the Dreader first swam to the Isle of Berk, Hiccup Horrendous Haddock the Third looked up at his father, Stoick the Vast, the Chief of the Hairy Hooligan Tribe.

'I think you're wrong, Father,' stammered Hiccup.

The Great Hall on Berk was full to bursting with Hooligan Warriors, slightly less large of belly and chunky of thigh than they had been six weeks before, but still an impressively gigantic and unwashed lot. This mass of muscled, hairy Vikings gave a gasp of horror and turned to gaze at Hiccup, who stood on one leg and turned red to the tips of his ears.

Hiccup was not what you might call a typical Hooligan.

He was thin and clever-looking, with the kind of entirely unmemorable face that

does not normally stick out in a crowd.
After six weeks of eating very little, he was
just skin and bone, and his elbows stuck
out of his shirt like sticks.

'Wrong?' bellowed Stoick the Vast.
'You think I'm WRONG????'

Stoick, on the other hand, although
Not-as-Vast-as-He-Normally-Was (owing to
the forced diet as a result of the
Dreader's presence), still had
muscles on his chest that would
have made a decent-sized bull
weep tears of jealousy.

And when he
bellowed, he
BELLOWED like a
dinosaur declaring war,
so these gentle words
could have been heard
faintly but clearly on
the neighbouring
island.

Hiccup
swallowed hard.

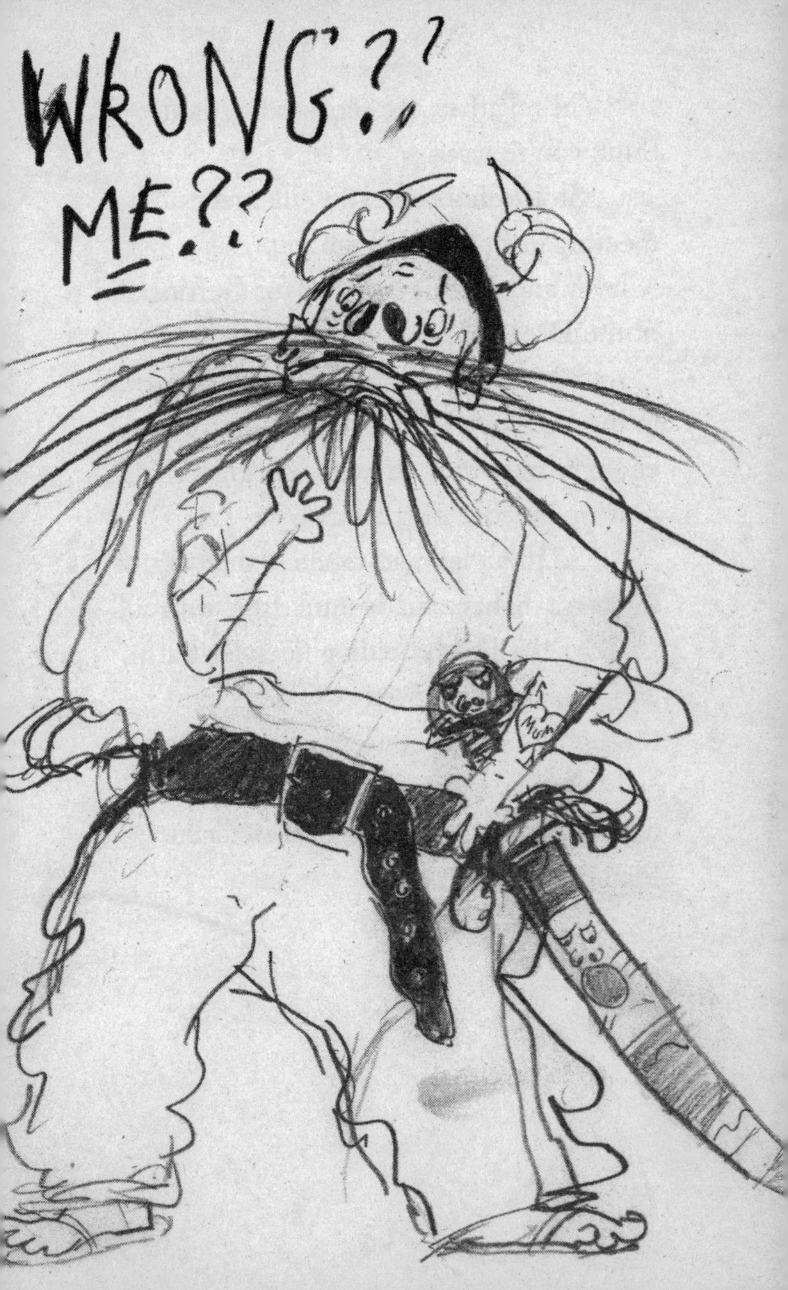
WRONG???
ME??

'Yes, Father,' he repeated defiantly. 'I think you're wrong.'

Stoick had called an emergency meeting in the Great Hall to present his 'Clever and Intelligent Plan for Getting Rid of the Dreader'.

Stoick was not the brightest barbarian in the business. In fact, he had just about enough brain-cells to keep one gigantic leg moving in front of the other.

So this Plan had taken him weeks of sleepless nights, and painful days, with Gobber the Belch holding his sword-arm and applying hot towels while he went through the exhausting process of thinking.

And as a result Stoick wasn't too happy about the Clever and Intelligent Plan being criticised.

The Plan was this:

'Stoik the VAST's
CLEVVER And
inTELLiJENT PLaN

1. Hole TriBe wakes erly
(to take CreetuRE by
surprize)

2. set sail, Bashing aXEs
on sheelds.
(to canFuse the creetuRE)

3. BasH the moNster
untill it dies or swimms
away.

4. SeLEbrate with larj
fish Feest and annual bankwet
to bee called from this
moment on : THE Day
of the Dredder

'If you provoke the Dreader like this, it might attack out of self-defence,' said Hiccup. 'I think we should try and talk to it, and ask it what it wants…'

'TALK TO IT?' yelled Stoick. 'The speaking of Dragonese is forbidden, as well you know. And Legend tells us that the Dreader is one of the most fearsome and supernatural creatures in the Archipelago. Its power is horrific…'

'Well then,' said Hiccup stubbornly, 'if we can't talk to it I think we should be patient a little longer, and wait for it to go away.'

Stoick the Vast swelled and turned purple with temper. 'BE PATIENT?' stormed Stoick the Vast furiously. 'I've been eating limpets for the last six weeks! If that's not patience, I don't know what is.'

'Yes, but Father—' argued Hiccup.

'SILENCE!' roared Stoick. 'The Chief has spoken! Every man, woman, child and dragon will join in the Clever and

Limpets were yucky!

Intelligent Plan tomorrow! The Dreader
must die!'

'**ATTACK!**' bellowed the Vikings,
raising weary arms despite their empty
tummies. 'The Dreader dies tomorrow!'

Fishlegs, Hiccup's best friend, was
the only person in the Hooligan Tribe who

was worse at everything Vikingy than Hiccup. Fishlegs had asthma, eczema, and an inconvenient allergy to reptiles.

Now he sighed, and said to Hiccup, 'You're not going to persuade them, Hiccup. You know what they're like. After a while they just have to go and BASH something, however stupid an idea that is. It's like asking a whole load of over-excited warthogs to be patient.'

FISHLEGS
(Hiccup's best friend)

Hiccup sighed too. 'I know, I just have a really bad feeling about this Dreader business.' Hiccup swallowed. His stomach did a couple of nauseating flip-flops as he thought about some of the things he had found out about the Dreader in the sagas he had read. 'I heard about one Viking ship that had a nasty encounter with a Dreader… and when they came back to Harbour –' Hiccup's voice dropped to a whisper '– every one of them had lost their heads. They were all sitting there, still holding their oars… but not a head on any of them. No wonder all the other dragons are frightened of them.'

Fishlegs sighed and rubbed his neck. 'I thought they were just supposed to send you mad. But they remove your whole head, do they? You see, I'm very fond of my head,' said Fishlegs. 'Me and my head go way back. Call me old-fashioned but I'm definitely keen on keeping it right where it is.'

Up in the rafters perched the hunting-dragons, large as crocodiles, their ribs showing through their thin skin, their eyes watching the cheering Vikings down below. There were Slitherfangs, Gronckles, Monstrous Nightmares – a multitude of dragon species. Who will win the day tomorrow? thought the dragons. Whoever it is, we shall get fed at last.

Dragons, you see, are only faithful to their human masters up to a certain point. And the dragons were hungry too.

Dreaders

~ STATISTICS ~

FEAR FACTOR: *10*
ATTACK: *10*
SPEED: *9*
SIZE: *10*
DISOBEDIENCE: *10*

Dreaders are one of the most feared Seadragons in the Archipelago. Great White Sharks and killer whales flee like flies at the first hint of a Dreader in their waters. Even the mighty Blue Whale is frightened of a Dreader. It is said that the Dreader sucks every drop of moisture from its victim's body, leaving it as thin as a piece of paper. Or the Dreader removes the head, or heart, or senses of the victim, leaving it mad as a box of frogs, or a lifeless lump of flesh.

2. WHO'S THE BOSS?

Later that evening, when Hiccup returned home, Stoick, his father, was furious with him.

'How dare you question me in public, Hiccup!' yelled Stoick. 'Criticising my plan, and banging on about talking to the Dreader, when everyone knows that the speaking of Dragonese is forbidden. Not only is it disloyal to me, it's dangerous. You will be Chief one day and you can't have them thinking you talk to dragons. It's not allowed and, well, it is a little… weird!'

Hiccup looked miserable. He was always trying to please his father, and somehow he never seemed to.

'Promise me you will not try and talk to this monster!' ordered Stoick. 'I don't want you getting too close to it!'

Hiccup mumbled that he promised.

'And another thing!' roared Stoick. 'Who do you think did this?'

Stoick held up the chewed remains of a swordbelt. *Uh-oh*.

Hiccup's hunting-dragon, Toothless, was hiding guiltily under the table.

Toothless was the smallest, cutest, most wriggly Common-or-Garden hunting-dragon that anybody had ever seen, before or since.

He was also the NAUGHTIEST.

'Umm…' muttered Hiccup. 'Mice?' he suggested hopefully.

'This was not mice! Those are the gum-marks of a fang-free dragon!' yelled Stoick. 'YOUR dragon, Hiccup! And I suppose you're going to tell me that those flame-breathing mice have set fire to my priceless spear collection as well?'

Toothless was hiding guiltily under a table.

'That dragon of yours is completely out of control!' screamed Stoick the Vast. 'If he's not chewing things, he's burning my underpants. There are scorch-marks all over this house. You have to show him who's boss, Hiccup, show him who's boss.'

And Stoick the Vast reached under the table with his big fat arm, and he caught Toothless by the leg, and sat him on the table.

'NOW LISTEN TO ME, JUICELESS OR WHATEVER YOU'RE CALLED,' yelled Stoick firmly. 'THE NEXT TIME YOU BURN SOMETHING OR CHEW SOMETHING I WILL THROW YOU OUT OF THIS HOUSE FOR EVER, DO YOU UNDERSTAND ME?

'You see, Hiccup?' explained Stoick. 'It's perfectly simple. I am your boss, so I think up the Clever and Intelligent Plan, and you do as you are told. And you are the boss of Toothless, so you tell him what to do and he does it. Now, I'm going to

need an early night
if I'm going to bash
up that Dreader
tomorrow.'

And he gave a gigantic
yawn and stomped off to bed.

Hiccup looked at Toothless
reproachfully.

'You have to stop being so selfish,'
said Hiccup.*

'But T-T-Toothless was hungry,'
whined Toothless. 'Was Toothless's
tummy's fault. It told Toothless it was so

---

*Hiccup was speaking to his dragon in Dragonese, for
Hiccup was one of the few Vikings, before or since, who
have been able to speak this fascinating language.

empty and Toothless
felt sorry for it...'

Hiccup sighed.

'We're all
hungry, Toothless.
It's so hard
looking after you if
you won't do what you're
told. You *know* the rules,
they're all written up on your star
chart... No chewing my father's stuff...'

'O-O-OK,' Toothless nodded his
head so hard his horns wobbled.

'No pooing inside the house...'

'N-n-n-no, no, no...' agreed
Toothless.

'And absolutely no setting fire to
things...' said Hiccup in his sternest voice.
'You don't want my father throwing you
out, do you?'

'Toothless will be g-g-good!' said
Toothless. 'Toothless promises. Cross
Toothless's heart and hope to die,
Toothless will be very, very good.'

But I'm afraid I know the truth, and
Toothless had his claws crossed behind
his back.

Learning to Speak Dragonese

Being Polite

TOOTHLESS: (to Snotlout and Fireworm)

Yow issa f-f-fishface ickle pinkywriggle wi na scrapers and yow Yellfatter has a sniffer too giganticus, yow may goggla sa fra da starrybit Mars.

You are an ugly little worm with no claws and your Master has a nose so large you could see it from the planet Mars.

HICCUP: (to Toothless)

Make sweetispeek, Toothless! Make sweetispeek! Be polite Toothless! Be polite!

TOOTHLESS: (to Hiccup)

Quera Toothless make sweetispeek toodi nobrainy greenclaw un Yellfatter meansters?

Why should Toothless be polite to that stupid horrible dragon and his Master?

HICCUP: (to Toothless)

Parsk undiless di nobrainy greenclaw and di nobrainy Yellfatter wull scrape us toodi big dreamtime.

Because otherwise they're going to KILL us.

Toothless hiding
under the covers

3. A LITTLE SNACK FOR TOOTHLESS

The next day, the Hooligans got ready for war against the Dreader, and Toothless refused to go.

'Is not Toothless's fault that big bully Dreader is in the Harbour. Nothing to do with Toothless,' Toothless sniffed from under the nice warm covers.

'OK,' said Hiccup, 'you stay here if you don't want to help, but DON'T LEAVE THIS ROOM, TOOTHLESS. My father is cross enough with you already.'

Hiccup looked very silly in his battle kit. He was now so skinny his belt kept slipping down over his hips and tripping him up.

'T-T-Toothless do as he's told. Toothless a good dragon,' said Toothless. 'N-n-no chewing, n-n-no pooing, no burning, Toothless knows...'

But as soon as Toothless heard Hiccup's footsteps padding out the front door, and the sound of those Hooligans thundering down the hillside towards the Harbour, Toothless poked out his snout from under the covers.

'P-p-poor Toothless is hungry,' he moaned. 'Nobody cares about poor Toothless starving to death. They all so s-s-selfish...' Toothless's fat little belly gave a protesting rumble, as if in agreement. Toothless patted it comfortingly. 'D-d-don't you worry, lovely little tummy... Toothless'll feed you... You can rely on Toothless...'

He gave a sudden squeal of excitement. He had just remembered. A couple of months ago, he had buried three eggs just outside the Great Hall. Toothless often hid little snacks like this, so that he could enjoy them at a later date, but with all the excitement about the Dreader he had completely forgotten about this particular little treat.

Toothless swooped through the smoke in the empty hall and out through the open door. There was a scrabbly patch of grass and gorse bushes and bracken in front of the Great Hall, and Toothless flew over it several times, his sharp little greengage eyes searching for something. Eventually he found the right spot, and started digging vigorously with his front paws.

The ferns shook maniacally for a couple of minutes, mud spraying upwards like a dirt volcano, until Toothless unearthed three large eggs, a beautiful lime green in colour, and lightly speckled with pale-brown freckles. Toothless licked his lips with his forked tongue, mouth watering already. FOOD.

There was nothing Toothless liked more than a delicious egg. Boiled eggs, fried eggs, coddled eggs, you name it, Toothless liked them any way at all.

But Toothless was particularly fond of a *baked* egg, cooked for just long enough that the yoke was still runny but the white was firm and scrumptious.

Toothless began to roll the eggs towards the open door of the Great Hall, using the end of his snout and his wings. It was quite tricky rolling three of them at once, as they tended to go off in opposite directions, and he had to be very gentle, for fear of cracking them. Once he'd got them through the front door it was easier, for the Great Hall had a smooth dirt floor, just right for rolling. Triumphantly, Toothless rolled the eggs over the floor, and one, two, three, *right* into the ashes of the fire smoking on the hearthstone.

Then, cooing with greed, he tenderly scooped the ash over them with his wings, so that they were completely buried in the hot grey dust. (Toothless's skin, like all dragonskin, was fairly fireproof, so he could do this without hurting himself.)

Chirruping with satisfaction, and drooling with excitement, Toothless perched on one leg on top of the meat-spit, to wait for them to cook, blinking fondly at the little mounds in the ash.

one ... two .... three

dragon eggs.

4. IS THERE SUCH A THING AS A HAUNTED EGG?

After about two minutes, something strange happened.

The ash around the eggs turned lime-green, and the eggs themselves began to shake, and one of them shook so hard that it wobbled itself right out of the ash and rolled on to the floor again. Squeaking with alarm, Toothless shepherded it back into the ash again, muttering, 'N-n-not ready yet! You're not ready!'

But no sooner had he got one egg safely back and buried in the ash, then another rolled off in a completely different direction. Squealing and baffled, Toothless swooped after one, and then the other, scooping them back into the fire with his wings, like an anxious mother hen with her disobedient chicks. But they kept on rolling out again, and before long Toothless

was out of breath, and indignant and covered with ash.

Finally, he manoeuvred one of the eggs all the way back from the other side of the room for the fifth time, and buried it lovingly next to its fellows, and there was a brief moment when all three lay still, as they should be. 'Th-th-there,' said Toothless with a grunt of satisfaction – and all three gave a violent tremble at the same

time, as if they were in
secret communication with
one another, and rocked
fiercely out of the fire-bed, bowling around
the room in wild wandering circles.

Toothless sat down heavily in the fire,
in his bewilderment, putting out the last
remains of the flames with his bottom. He
followed the lunatic progress of the eggs
with his eyes as they looped crazily around
the dust of the Great Hall, gathering speed
as they went.

'W-w-what's going on?' squeaked
Toothless. 'Stay h-h-here and do as you're
told!'

Food shouldn't run away like this. It
should stay still, and let itself be cooked,

like any self-respecting sausage or carrot. It shouldn't be running around the room as if it had a mind of its own, weaving its way through the chair legs and generally showing off.

One of the eggs had come to rest against a table leg. Crouching down low, Toothless stalked the egg slowly, as if it were prey. The egg did not move. Feeling braver, Toothless edged a little closer. The egg remained motionless. Toothless froze, ready to pounce, whiskers quivering faintly, every muscle tense. The egg was egg-ily still.

Toothless sprang... and just at the last minute the egg wobbled wildly to life, swerving out of the way and skittering out of reach, so that poor Toothless's paws closed on nothing, and the momentum carried him forward, and he bashed his nose on the table leg.

'Rrreeeowww...' Toothless let out a strangled meowing nose like a cat that has had its tail pulled.

And '*Tee-hee-hee-hee-hee...*' came the sound from the egg, gently vibrating on the spot. Toothless could have sworn it was tittering. Muffled giggling noises came from the two other eggs, on the other sides of the room.

Now poor Toothless was thoroughly terrified. He stuck his tail between his legs and whimpered pathetically.

'*H-H-H-HAUNTED* eggs!' moaned poor Toothless. Probably inhabited by the ghosts of vengeful suppers that Toothless had burgled over the years, and let's face it, there were loads of those.

It was the only explanation. Just as he was backing away, the spines on his back quivering like porcupine needles, there was a loud CRACK!

… and crooked little lines appeared all over the lime-green surface of the egg.
CRACK! CRACK! CRACK!

A hard little head punched its way through the egg-shell (it had to be hard for the shells of dragon eggs are nearly a centimetre thick). A tiny little dragon, with huge yellow eyes and a black smudge on the end of its nose, blinked back at an astonished Toothless.

And after a gob-smacked minute while Toothless digested this latest surprising development:

'Papa!' squeaked the little smudgy dragon. 'Papa! Papa! Papa!'

5. TOOTHLESS IS NOT YOUR PAPA

With every 'Papa!' the tiny creature head-butted the shell that was still partly encasing him, until with a final CRACK! the dragon unfolded its wet little wings and the egg fell apart entirely into tiny smashed pieces of green.

The dragon was far smaller than the size of the egg that had encased it, a little larger perhaps than a baby chick or duckling, but not a lot. It was covered all over with lime-green goo, and as it shook out its wings, the startling orange of a scallop coral, it flung a fine rain of gooey stuff over Toothless himself.

'Y-y-yucky,' groaned Toothless.

The little dragon grinned. 'Papa,' it repeated, looking up at him lovingly.

Toothless was horrified. 'Me? Toothless not your P-p-papa. Toothless HATES babies...'

The dragon baby ignored this and hopped towards Toothless enthusiastically. 'Papa!'

CRACK! CRACK! CRACK!

The other two eggs split apart too, on opposite sides of the room.

'Papa!'

'Papa!'

Two more little dragon babies hopped out of the smashed remains of their shells and hopped unsteadily towards Toothless.

The second one was yellow rather than green and had a remarkably flat head, because it had spent its egg-hood bashing against the walls of the shell. The third was a bit smaller and bright blue and kept on falling over because it had a rather wobbly leg, and a permanent case of the hiccups.

one... two... three

little dragons

It tended to
charge ahead in an
uncontrolled fashion as if its legs
had run away with it, before listing to the
left and landing on its bottom and saying
'Whoops!' in a surprised fashion. Although
why it was surprised I have no idea,
because it fell over pretty much every two
minutes, so it shouldn't have been much of
a shock when it did it again.

It also had a terrible cold, so every
now and then it added 'Aaatishoo!' to the
'Hic!', 'Whoops' and 'Ow!'s.

'Papa!' squealed the second one
gruffly.

'It's our Papa! Hic! Whoops... Ow...
ATISHOO!' said the third one.

'Toothless N-N-NOT your Papa,'
said Toothless firmly, but backing away
nonetheless as the little creatures rushed
towards him in a flurry of green goo.

'Toothless not like babies...

B-b-babies is yucky and wet, and ever so soppy...'

These babies were certainly all that, but they carried on rushing towards him in a yucky soppy gooey mess nonetheless, and he had to take off suddenly so that the little blue one bashed into all the others, and Toothless flapped up to perch on one of the ceiling beams and blinked down at them furiously. They couldn't yet fly, so they couldn't follow him, they just leapt up and down, cheeping and clicking furiously.

Toothless tucked his head under his wing and pretended to go to sleep.

Five minutes later they were still there, cheeping and clicking, and bouncing more hysterically than ever.

'Papa! Papa! Papa!'

Oh, fish-hooks.

Toothless would never live it down with the

little GREEN dragon   little YELLOW dragon   little BLUE dragon.

other dragons if he kept on being followed about by soppy little dragon babies.

'GO AWAY! Toothless NOT your Papa...Toothless just tried to eat you... Toothless could *still* eat you...' Toothless shouted down from the roof beam.

In fact, Toothless ate pretty much anything but even *he* drew the line at baby dragons who thought you were their father. However, from Toothless's perch he had a great view out of one of the high windows.

Through the window, he caught sight of a red dragon flying towards the house, still some distance away.

Fireworm.

Fireworm would take care of the problem. You see, Fireworm was a Monstrous Nightmare and did not suffer from any of Toothless's rare qualms of conscience, and she would gobble up three insufferably cute little dragons in less time than it took a dragon to scratch its own ear. The cuter the better, as far as Fireworm was concerned.

Toothless grinned. She was definitely flying their way, probably hoping that Stoick had left some titbits over from breakfast. Toothless settled down more comfortably on the roof beam to wait for her to show up. It wouldn't be *his* fault if Fireworm decided to eat them, would it?

The moment that Fireworm set eyes on those babies, they would be doomed…

6. THE TERRIBLE POWER OF THE DREADER

I'm sorry, it doesn't seem a very good moment, but we'll just have to leave those babies in awful peril, about to be eaten up by Fireworm, while we return to catch up with what was happening with Hiccup and the Hooligans.

Because they were in trouble too, you see.

Dreadful, ghastly trouble.

Trouble too nasty to even *think* about, let alone tell.

The Hooligans were aboard their ships, and the ships were

already out in the bay, carrying out Stoick's Clever and Intelligent Plan.

They were advancing on that great, grim underwater shadow, banging on their shields with their axes to shoo away this terrible beast.

Even the bravest of the Hooligans, magnificent warriors like that gormless muscly giant, Gobber the Belch, were terrified, and white to the lips.

All of their senses told them to 'Go back!', to run away from that darkness under the waves, and not to go nearer.

'Go back! Go back! Go back!'

But hunger had made them desperate.

So they *forced* their quaking hairy arms to row towards the dreadful shadow.

They *made* their poor exhausted limbs bash those axes weakly on those shields, and *ordered* their poor shaking feet to drum out a pathetic human warning to the mighty, pitiless horror that was lurking under the water.

It was very, very brave of those Hooligans.

It was also extremely stupid.

Hiccup and Fishlegs were aboard Stoick's ship, *The Fat Penguin*.

Fishlegs was trembling all over, his legs shivering uncontrollably, as if he had caught some feverish plague. He had his eyes closed, in the useless and pathetic hope that if he couldn't *see* what was happening, maybe he wasn't really there.

He tried to bash his axe on his shaking shield, moaning, 'Oh this noise really isn't helping my headache one bit...'

Fishlegs laughed, but the laugh grew out of control, and became a bit hysterical. 'What's going on, Hiccup? Has the Dreader sucked out anybody's heart or

Oh... this noise isn't helping my headache ONE BIT.

removed their head yet?'

'Not yet,' replied Hiccup cautiously. He too, was pale as death, heart beating so quick he felt sick with the pulse of it. This was going to be a really unpleasant way to die...

And then, in front of Hiccup's terrified eyes, a miracle happened.

'Hang on a second,' panted Hiccup, in joyous astonishment. 'I don't believe it... It's turning... It's moving away!'

And so it seemed. The dark shape uncurled its serpentine coils from around the island. It moved away, out into the sea that was Woden's Bathtub, and as it moved, the famished Vikings could hardly believe their luck.

Terror turned to hope in an instant.

The hope gave strength to their arms, and they increased their banging on the shields and let out a ragged Hooligan Hoorah, as they saw themselves being able to fish for food for the first time in many, many weeks.

'Bring out the nets!' bellowed Stoick the Keen-to-be-Vast-Again, red with relief.

Thank Thor, thank Thor.

For one horrible moment, he had thought perhaps his Plan hadn't been such a good one after all. He shook his sword, and patted his poor empty belly.

'You see, Hiccup?' Flushed and beaming with triumph, Stoick turned to his son. 'The Plan is working, my boy.'

He patted Hiccup kindly on the head. 'Watch and learn, Hiccup laddie, watch and learn. My Clever and Intelligent Plan is working. Thinking skills, you see. Brain power.'

Stoick tapped his hairy head importantly, and then roared to the Viking warriors in relieved joy: 'THERE WILL BE FEASTING TONIGHT, BY THE STOMACH-JUICES OF THOR, THERE WILL, MY FELLOW HOOLIGANS!'

But WHO would be feasting on WHOM???

Sometimes we rejoice too soon, brothers and sisters.

Sometimes we rejoice too soon, and

we forget we are not safe until we reach the shore, or the end of the story, whichever is nearer.

It seemed that the Hooligans *had* rejoiced too soon, for slowly, slowly the shadow that had been moving away, like a departing underwater battleship, slowly, slowly, came to a halt.

Slowly, slowly, the shadow turned again…

It turned to face the Hooligan fleet.

Stoick was not what you might call a lightning thinker, but even *he* realised that this was not good news. His mouth dropped open. 'Uh-oh.'

And the Hooligan Hurrah died on famished lips, and all around the ships the Hooligans stopped banging on their shields, and the noise came to a confused halt as their poor weakened arms were frozen in terror.

All except for Fishlegs, who banged away more shakily than ever, squeaking, 'Why are they stopping, Hiccup? Why are

CLANG!

CLANG!

CLANG!

they stopping? Actually don't tell me... I don't want to know.'

Hiccup, peering out into that darkness, swallowed hard, though his mouth had no moisture, for it was dry as dust.

'Don't open your eyes yet, Fishlegs,' was all he said.

The shadow was moving...

Oh for Thor's sake, it was huge…

It was moving, moving, and the darkened sea swelled up and began to surge towards them like a tidal wave but it wasn't a tidal wave at all…

It was the Dreader.

7. THE ATTACK OF THE DREADER

There was a dreadful ghastly silence.

And then the Hooligans lost it.

Relief turned back to terror again, in an instant.

They forgot their empty bellies, and their pride, and the Clever and Intelligent Plan.

All they saw was the shadow, that hole in the water that they filled up with their worst, their darkest, their most terrible fears...

And then 'MAKE FOR THE SHORE!' bellowed Stoick the Vast, and they hauled on the sail like wild things, trying to change direction and go back to the harbour, for the wind was carrying them straight into the path of the charging beast.

Only Fishlegs banged away madly at his shield, eyes tight shut, shouting, 'Don't tell me what's happening! Don't tell me what's happening!'

But Hiccup couldn't have told him what was happening anyway.

Hiccup, you see, had forgotten the promise that he had made his father.

He was already leaning over the side of the boat, shouting at the Dreader in the water, the shadow that was gaining on them...

Just to make things even worse, the wind had died.

The sail was flapping and sagging uselessly as the Dreader stormed towards them.

It was as if they were in one of those bad dreams in which you are being chased, but you cannot move your legs.

The boat was stuck to the ocean like a fly to fly-paper.

The Vikings blundered towards their oars, roaring in terror, pushing each other over in their panic.

Hiccup leaned as far as he could over

the side of the boat.

'WHAT... DO... YOU... WANT?' shouted Hiccup at the Dreader in Dragonese. 'HOW... CAN... I... HELP YOU?'

The tiny words were snatched by the wind the moment they left Hiccup's mouth.

DO YOU WANT?

Snatched, and
tossed away, as the
depression in the water deepened and
gained and the wind screamed louder.

Hiccup HAD to get close to this
dragon, so that he could speak to it. He
just HAD to...

Thinking of nothing but getting near
enough so his voice could be heard,
Hiccup climbed the slippery dragon
figure-head of the boat, his hands sliding
on the cold wet wood, the wind tearing
maniacally at his clothes and his hair.

'WHAT DO YOU WANT??'
screamed Hiccup, louder still. 'Please
don't take our heads... or our
blood, or our hearts... WHAT
DO YOU WANT???'

And then right in front of Hiccup's
terrified gaze, two enormous eyes rose to

the surface, but did not break the water.

'AAAAAARRGGHHGHHHH!' shrieked Hiccup, as to his absolute horror, his hands slid on the wooden dragon's head. He couldn't keep his grip. He was going to fall into the sea, into the path of that dreadful creature.

He fell...

... and the back of his waistcoat caught on the edge of one of the figurehead's teeth, so that he hung there, dangling and scrabbling wildly in front of the advancing Dreader, like a fish on a hook.

Oh for Thor's sake, shrieked a voice in Hiccup's head. *I'm going to be the first to go...*

He braced himself for the Dreader's attack.

The mouth broke the water, and the creature screamed as if in pain. The wind from its inhaling mouth sucked the boat towards it, despite the Vikings desperately paddling with all the strength of their hungry limbs.

The inhaled scream of that
Dreader made the head ring from the
inside, as if it was a bell being rung by
Thor's hammer, but it seemed to Hiccup
like the weird terrible scream contained
half-formed words in a very ancient
Dragonese indeed, and the words were:

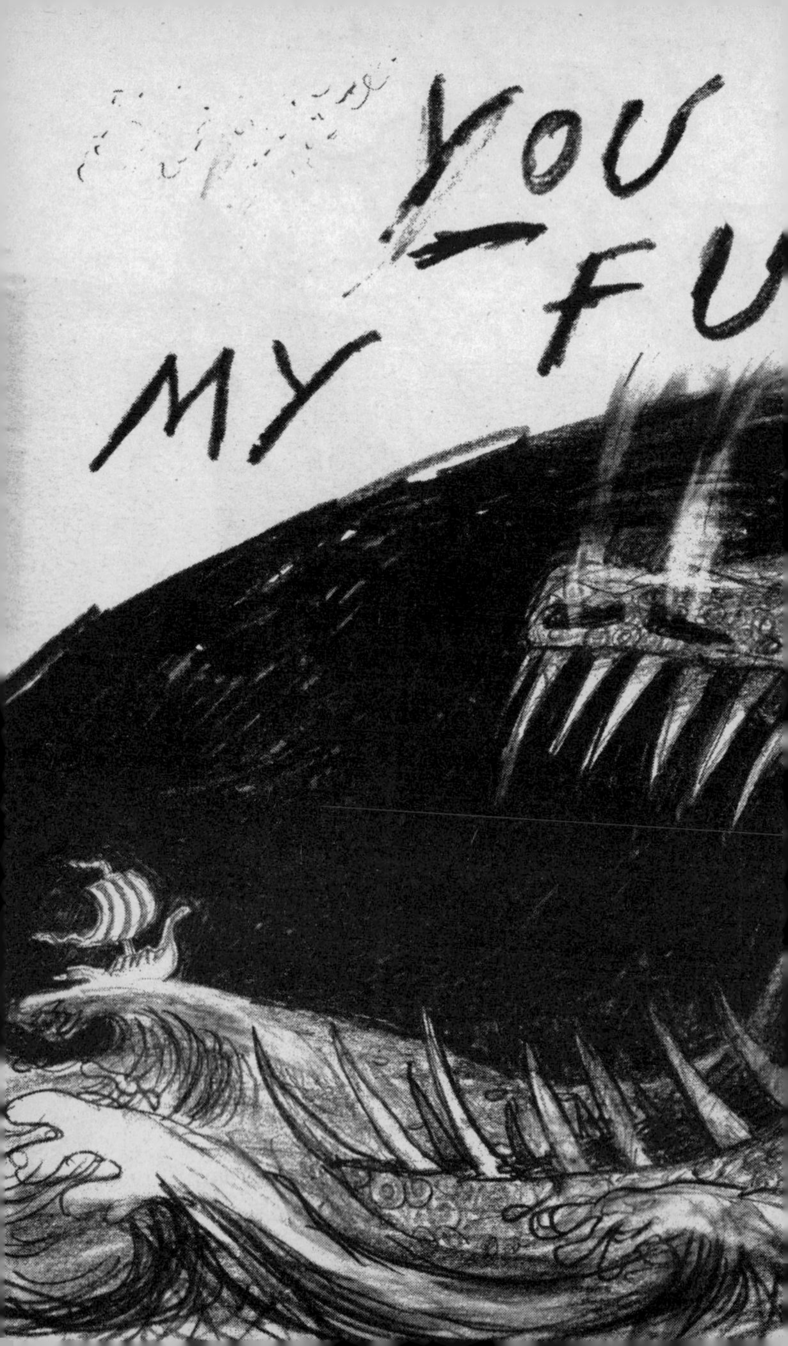
YOU
MY
FU

STOLE
TURE...

Maybe that was what the words were, and maybe that wasn't – they were so unformed it was hard to say.

But on the final shrieking syllable the sucking-in ceased and the creature exhaled, and Hiccup's last thought was:

Here we go... The Dreader's going to use its power now...

And there was a truly ear-splitting noise... A horrible choking yank at Hiccup's neck...

I'm going to die, thought Hiccup.

And everything went black.

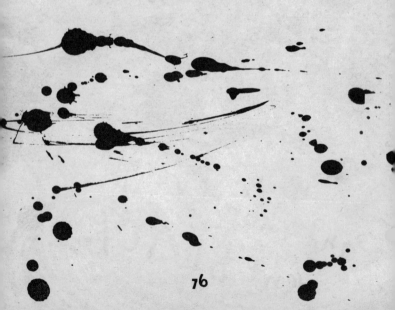

... and then everything went BLACK.

8. DRAGONS ARE SELFISH, DON'T YOU KNOW THAT?

Now I'm afraid this doesn't seem a good moment to leave Hiccup EITHER, does it, given that he's about to die?

But we just have to catch up with those cute and helpless dragon babies whom we left moments away from a messy death in the jaws of Fireworm.

This is all very inconvenient but we can't leave the poor little things for one second longer.

You see the problem with story telling? Sometimes so many things are going on at once you can't keep up with everything at the same time.

We had left Fireworm flying towards the open door of Hiccup's house, and as soon as she set eyes on those dragon babies, they would be EX-dragon babies, sure as fish-eggs are fish-eggs.

Toothless was watching from the roof
beam above, delighted that the
problem of the little pests was
going to be taken out of his
paws, because their
unbelievably
high-pitched
chirping was
giving him a
headache.

'Papa!
Papa! Papa!'
squeaked the
babies. 'We love
you, Papa!'
Toothless
snorted disgustedly.

Papa is wonderful... HIC ...whoops...

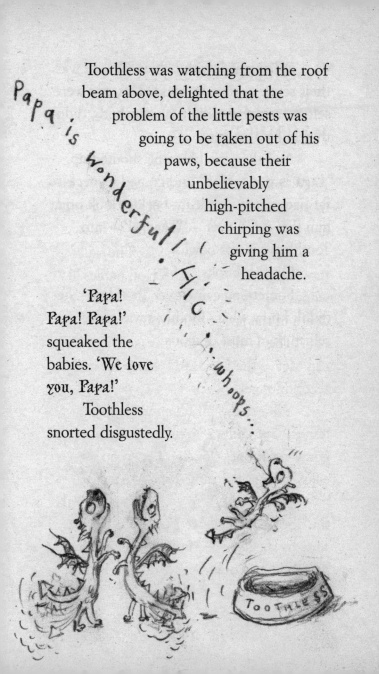

What was it with babies? Where was their sense of dragon-hood? Dragons were selfish, and they didn't love anybody, didn't they know that yet?

And then the blue one shouted up, 'Papa is wonderful!' and craned its neck so far backwards as it leant back to look up at him that it fell over – 'Whoops!' – into Toothless's water bowl.

Oh fish-hooks.

Something came over Toothless – he didn't know what. Toothless was more selfish than most dragons.

... splosh.

But whatever it was, it seemed Toothless couldn't let Fireworm eat the wretched little babies after all.

Quick as a diving falcon, he swooped down, plucked the blue one out of the water bowl with his mouth, the yellow one and the green one in each of his front paws, and carried them in a rain of goo and water up to the roof beam.

'B-b-be quiet!' he hissed at them fiercely, 'or you will DIE!'

'Oooh... Papa so brave,' they all cooed.

'Oh f-f-f-fiddlesticks,' sighed Toothless, his empty tummy grumbling even louder as he dived down again, panting, and perched on Stoick's chair-back, trying to look unconcerned.

In the nick of time.

In through the open door swooped the lean red panther body of Fireworm, a beautiful Monstrous Nightmare dragon, all gleaming muscles and glinting fangs. By some instinct, the squeaking from the roof

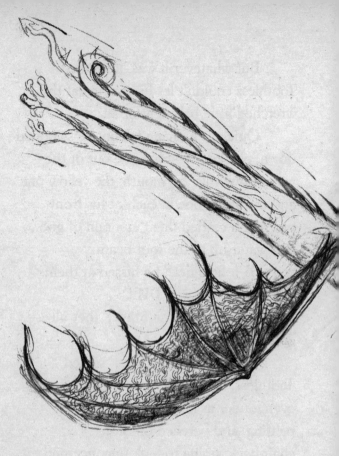

beam ceased instantly the moment she entered. She glided slowly round the room, like a gigantic malevolent red bat sensing drama, before landing on the hall floor and sharpening her talons on the bright edge of Stoick's axe.

'What has been going on here?' she
hissed at Toothless, looking suspiciously
round the room, taking in Toothless's
blackened state, covered in charcoal and
goo. Her serpent eyes brightened as she
saw the lime-green slime dripped liberally

all over the place, and the spilt water bowl, and the thousands and thousands of pieces of smashed lime-green dragon egg.

'Babies?' she purred, licking her lips with her long forked tongue. 'Delicious soggy gooey little dragon babies? Oh how I love to wring their goggly little necks, the gooier the better! So, where are they, Toothless?'

So. Where are they, Toothless?

She pointed her pin-sharp front talon, long as a scimitar, right at Toothless's throat. 'I know you would want to share...'

'T-T-Toothless already ate them,' said Toothless rudely, as careless as he could be.

It was very believable, for Toothless was the greediest little dragon on Berk, and he was covered head to toe in lime-green goo.

Quick as lightning, the talon came down. Luckily Toothless was quicker still, and jumped out of the way just as it plunged into the chair, practically carving it in half.

'Savage!' hissed Fireworm. 'Greedy little mongrel!'

'You l-l-looking too fat, anyway, Fireworm!' jeered Toothless, sticking his forked tongue out at her.

Fireworm aimed a jet of flame at him, and again he dodged it. Nobody was better at dodging than Toothless.

Toothless thought quickly. He had to

get rid of her. 'There's more of 'em though,' he said, pointing his wing to the door. 'Out in the h-h-harbour...'

Fireworm's eyes lit up with greed.

'Watch your back, you inflated little flying toad,' she warned Toothless nastily, as she flew swiftly out the door, to look for more delicious little dragon babies to eat.

Toothless heaved a sigh of relief.

She was gone.

But Fireworm had only just left, when...

BAM!

The first baby fell out of the hiding-place.

It made no attempt to fly, just hit the floor with a sickening thud.

Screeching with alarm, terrified that it must have broken something, Toothless swooped down to it.

The baby gave Toothless an angelic smile. 'I is *fine*!' it squeaked. 'Don't worry!'

Oh, for Thor's sake... Toothless

collapsed with relief, and…

BAM!

BAM!

Toothless jumped a foot in the air as the two other little babies slammed to the floor as well.

'We is fine *too*!' they squeaked, squealing with laughter at Toothless's alarm.

Poor Toothless had barely got over the shock when the little dragons shot off (at extraordinary speed, considering they couldn't fly yet, and were waddling on little newborn feet) in three different directions, squealing: 'We is hungry, Papa, HUNGRY!'

'What are you doing????' cried Toothless in alarm. 'We have no food… Toothless promised he w-w-wouldn't make a mess… *What are you doing????*'

CHOMP! CHOMP! CHOMP! The little green one munched a huge chunk out of Stoick's chair leg. The little yellow one set fire to the chair, and the curtains, and

the cupboard. And—

'Hic... Whoops! Ow! ATISHOO!'

There was a mountainous clatter from the larder as the little blue one went through it like a tiny dragon tornado, sending pans and cauldrons flying in all directions and bowling out the door.

'S-S-STOP!' cried poor Toothless, trying to put out the fires and yelling at the top of his voice. 'STOP! NO CHEWING! NO P-P-POOING! NO BURNING! TOOTHLESS WILL BE IN SO MUCH TROUBLE! STOP!!!!!'

STOP! NO CHEWING! NO P-P-POOING! NO BURNING!!

To his passionate relief, and surprise, the three little dragon babies shot wobbly and obediently towards him. They came to a halt underneath him, looking up at him

with
their
huge baby
dragon eyes,
innocently
questioning.

'Oh, thank Thor,'
panted Toothless, and he put
on his most stern voice. 'You
m-m-must not burn
anything... or eat anything... or
make a mess... or T-T-Toothless
will be in BIG TROUBLE,
understand?'

The three little dragons looked
up at him.

'Papa is wonderful,' said the
little blue one.

'We promise we'll be good...'
said the little yellow dragon.

*But all three little dragons had
their claws crossed behind their backs.*

There was a slight pause.

And then the little blue one made a big pooey mess in the middle of the floor.

The smell was indescribable. How could something so small make such a huge stink?

And all three shrieked, 'But we is HUNGRY!'

And off they dashed in three separate directions again, raking up the floors with their little dragon talons, and setting fire to things. The little blue one was already in Stoick's bedroom attacking all the pillows in case they contained food, and giving himself a coughing fit as he choked on the feathers.

Toothless was beside himself...

'AAAAGH!' he yelled. 'STOP IT, YOU LITTLE H-H-HORRORS! STOP IT! TOOTHLESS'LL PUT BLACK MARKS ON ALL YOUR STAR CHARTS! TOOTHLESS'LL PUT YOU TO BED WITHOUT ANY DINNER! TOOTHLESS'LL... TOOTHLESS'LL–'

But whoever was the boss of those little dragons, it certainly wasn't Toothless. They took absolutely no notice whatsoever.

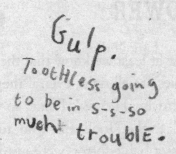

Gulp.
Toothless going to be in s-s-so much trouble.

9. BACK TO THE HOOLIGANS AND THE DREADER'S DREADFUL POWER

Now at least we know that the dragon babies are all right, even if they are destroying Hiccup's home, so we can go back to the Hooligans, who, to their indescribable terror, were just being attacked by the dread of the Dreader.

Oh, yes, and Hiccup was about to die, wasn't he?

I knew I'd forgotten something important.

Everything had gone black, and warm and wet, and there was a horrible choking feeling around Hiccup's neck.

'AAAAAARGGHH!' gargled Hiccup. 'AARRGH!'

For he thought he was about to lose his head, and maybe the warm-and-wetness——

was his own blood.

He was lifted upwards, as if by the arms of Thor himself, and he imagined that perhaps he was dead already, and being lifted up towards Valhalla?

The breath left his body with a sickening shock as he landed, sprawling and soaking wet, on some hard flat surface.

His eyes had closed automatically, but now he opened them, slowly and stickily, for it was like they had been dipped in glue. His heart was palpitating with fear like a rabbit's, for he thought he was opening his eyes into the next world.

But the hard flat surface he had landed on was in fact the wet wooden boards of the deck of *The Fat Penguin*, awash with some strange liquid substance much thicker than water.

Oh thank Thor.

He wasn't dead after all.

Yet.

Gasping, he looked upwards through his gummy eyelids.

That choking feeling around his neck must have been caused by Stoick hauling him by the back of the waistcoat over the edge of the boat. For Stoick was standing over him, gasping in shock, covered in a strange liquid blackness, his white eyes the only colour showing through.

All around the Vikings were screaming, 'MAKE FOR THE SHORE!' paddling like crazy, covered in this weird shiny blackness and spattering little liquid splats as they shovelled their way through the heaving sea.

The Hooligans did not stop to ask what had happened. They paddled like madmen for the shore, and it was only when they had landed all the boats in the harbour and staggered, dripping blackness, on to the beach, that they began to wonder what had gone on.

'Gobber…' said Stoick the Vast in a baffled, liquid sort of way, blowing bubbles through the goo that had gathered in his beard. 'Gobber… what *is* this stuff? We seem to be alive, but this stuff is very…'

'*Smelly*…' Hiccup pointed out.

For now that the terror of the moment had passed, the smell crept up on them, a smell so appalling that the inside of the nostrils burned like acid. It was a smell so much worse than anything you've ever smelt before. Imagine a skinful of skunks who had been taking a lot of exercise without using deodorant. Imagine rotten eggs and stinking haddock and rotting corpses and Baggybum's socks after he's been playing Bashyball for a couple of weeks, and you still haven't got there.

It was a smell so bad that it almost had a physical presence, as if a large dead wet walrus was hanging right in front of your nose.

'Stinkdragon,' panted Hiccup in wonder. 'The Dreader is just a giant Stinkdragon.'

'Hang on a second,' roared Stoick furiously. 'The Dreader's power, the power of Legend that has kept us hungry and eating nothing but limpets for the last six weeks, is *supposed* to be the power of removing people's heads! Or at the VERY LEAST it's meant to send you mad, or suck out your blood until you're flat as a piece of paper… Are you telling me that this power the Sagas have been going on about for centuries is not any of these things, it's just a *BAD SMELL????*'

'It looks like it,' said Hiccup. 'Legends do not always tell the truth. I guess if you're telling a Saga, a bad smell doesn't make such a good story.'

'Well, you have to admit, it's not just a light pong,' said Fishlegs. 'This is the worst smell I have ever smelt in my entire life. I can feel one of my rashes coming on.'

'I'LL NEVER BELIEVE A STORY AGAIN!' yelled Stoick, punching his fist in the air. 'THIS IS AN OUTRAGE!'

For a moment it looked like Stoick would explode.

Which would have been a messy business, what with all that yucky smelly black stuff all around. But instead his shoulders began to shake. Stinky little droplets showered off him like smelly rain, as Stoick the Vast, O Hear his Name and Tremble, threw back his gooey black head

and roared with laughter.

And then all the other Hooligans joined in: HA! HA! HA! HA! HA! Laughing fit to bust a gut, smelling to high heaven. No one can laugh like a Hooligan can laugh, great gusting belly laughs, even when those bellies are empty.

'RIGHTO GUYS!' bellowed Stoick. 'Let's clean this stuff off, and go out and catch ourselves some FISH!'

'Yes but, Father,' argued Hiccup, 'the Dreader is still out there, and he's still gigantically enormous even if his dreadful power IS only the power of pong –'

Stoick was suddenly serious again.

'Yes, you're right, Hiccup,' he said, scratching his head, and frowning. 'This calls for another of my Clever and Intelligent Plans.'

Hiccup sighed. It could take WEEKS while the wheels of Stoick's brain moved infinitely slowly to come up with something as ridiculous as the last Clever and Intelligent Plan. But Hiccup had more urgent problems.

For out of the corner of his eye he could see flames shooting upwards on the hillside, right in the heart of the Hooligan village.

His father's house was on fire.

Toothless. Oh for Thor's sake, what had Toothless done now?

As everyone else jumped in the Harbour, trying to scrub off the smelly stuff, **SQUELCH! SQUELCH! SQUELCH!** Dripping and reeking, Hiccup shot up the hill.

10. HAVING YOUR OWN PET IS A WONDERFUL THING OF COURSE

SQUELCH! SQUELCH! SQUELCH!
Hiccup was holding his own nose to try
and keep out the disgusting stench as he
half staggered, half ran up the hill, his legs
wide apart because the revolting
Dreader-juice was sloshing around the
inside of his trousers.

Bits of ferns and heather stuck to the
stuff as he fell flat on his face, and
staggered to his feet, and flung open the
broken door of his father's home.

'AAAAAGHHHHHHHH!'

How could one small dragon cause so
much devastation in so short a time?
Furniture, crockery, weapons smashed,
tables in flames, kitchenware scattered
across the length of the room – it was
as if a gang-load of fire-eating Berserks
had been charging around the place

on rhino-back.

'TOOOOOOTHLESSS!!!!!!'
howled Hiccup, without really expecting
the little dragon to reply, but Toothless
swooped down from the rafters, in
passionate relief, only just stopping himself
from landing on his Master's sticky black
head in time.

Toothless was in tears.

'They w-w-won't do anything
T-t-toothless says!' wailed Toothless
desperately.

'What are you talking about?'
screamed Hiccup. 'My father is going to
kill us, and then he'll throw you out, and
then he'll kill me again, and he was in
such a good mood—'

Toothless pointed a tragic wing
downwards. 'They did this! They
ch-ch-chewed everything, and they set
f-f-fire to everything, and they pooed
everywhere, and they w-w-wouldn't listen
to Toothless and it's... ALL... THEIR...
FAULT...'

Blinking through the stinking Dreader-goo, Hiccup looked down at his feet.

Three tiny little baby dragons were sitting in a row, one green, one yellow, one blue.

'Where did these dragons come from, Toothless?' asked Hiccup in a bewildered sort of way.

'Ah,' Toothless looked guilty. 'T-t-toothless found them... They hatched... From some eggs that t-t-turned up... Toothless was just out in the Open Ocean a couple of months ago, you see, and he found this little island, and these eggs were just l-l-lying there... Didn't seem to belong to anybody...'

'Toothless I keep telling you not to steal dragon eggs, you never know what type of dragon they might be!' exploded Hiccup.

Now the little dragons turned into little hissing spitting demons as they rushed to defend Toothless, who they thought was their father, against this horrible great big human who was being mean to him.

'Be nice to Papa!' spat the green one.

'Papa is wonderful!' said the yellow one.

And 'Hic... Whoops... Atishoo!' said the blue. And he opened up his little blue dragon mouth, and he inhaled with a little sucking noise, and then he exhaled, and out shot a little shower of black liquid.

It missed Hiccup's right foot by some distance.

The smell of it was extraordinary. How could something so tiny make a pong of such indescribable awfulness? A smell of rotting corpses, of stinking eggs, of dead wet walrus hanging in front of your nose...

AHA.

Suddenly everything fell into place.

Those eggs had just been lying there, had they? Somewhere out in the Open Ocean...

Hiccup bent down, scooped up the three little dragons in his arms, and shot off down the hill.

11. IT'S A MYSTERY

Down the hill, Hiccup ran, **SQUELCH! SQUELCH! SQUELCH!**, with the little dragons shrieking, and biting and squealing, 'Papa save us! Papa save us!' all the way down.

SQUELCH! SQUELCH! SQUELCH! Hiccup ran past the roaring, laughing Hooligans, still trying to scrub off the smell in the Harbour.

Into his boat, *The Hopeful Puffin*, Hiccup jumped, and he wrapped the little dragons in his dripping waistcoat to confuse them and set the sails out to the dark shadow beyond the Harbour.

He sailed out to where it was waiting, and then he shelved the oars, and drew out the little dragons, who bit him furiously.

'Papa save us! Papa save us!'

'HERE,' said Hiccup, 'This is your REAL Papa...'

And he dropped them one, two, over

the side. The third, the little blue one, had got a tight hold of Hiccup's trousers with his little jaws, and Hiccup had to work them free, and then he dropped him over the side as well, with a 'Hic... Whoops... Atish~' SPLASH!

They swam instantly underwater, a flash of yellow, green and blue, and the dark shadow shimmered under the water, and they were gone.

Hiccup could not see what was happening. No doubt explanations were going on under the water, but nothing could be heard.

There was silence.

Toothless was hovering over Hiccup's head. 'What are you d-d-doing?' he squeaked, furious, outraged. 'That D-d-dreader is out there... The Dreader will get them...'

'The Dreader is their... Papa,' explained Hiccup sternly. 'Or parent, anyway.'

'N-n-no!' exclaimed Toothless.

'Where did you find those eggs, Toothless? Those were the Dreader's eggs, and who could blame it if it came looking for its eggs? I have told you and told you, Toothless, not to go stealing eggs. And now you know why.'

Toothless denied everything, swore he had come upon the eggs entirely by accident. But both he and Hiccup knew the truth of the matter.

And then far, far out in the Bay, way, way in the distance, as it swam to the Open Sea, the gigantic form of the Dreader LAUNCHED itself out of the water.

It was just a glimpse of this creature that never allowed itself to be seen by man, but what a magnificent sight it was, impossibly huge, a breathtaking green, not dreadful at all.

Hiccup caught his breath at the wonder of it. And was it Hiccup's imagination, or was the flipper raised in a sort of salute?

And was that three little specks, diving after it, squeaking joyously?

On the wind, the faint words in ancient Dragonese:

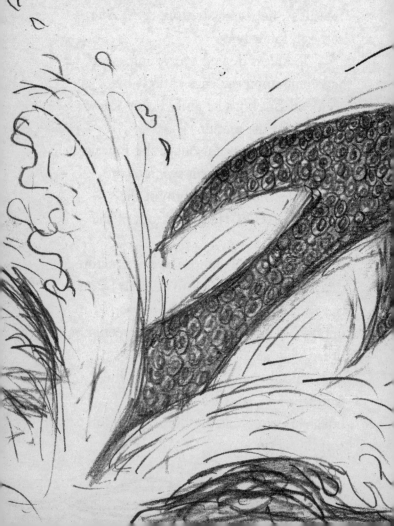

'THANK YOU...'

Toothless sniffed.

'Toothless'll miss them... They're smelly and n-n-naughty, but so *cute*... How can little dragon babies that cute grow up to be big fat Dreaders?'

'I don't know, Toothless,' said Hiccup shaking his head. 'It's a mystery.'

Hiccup sailed *The Hopeful Puffin* back to the Harbour, and called out to the Hooligan Warriors, who had done the best they could to wash themselves, to say that the Dreader was gone.

'Excellent,' boomed Stoick the Vast, rubbing his hands together, deeply relieved he didn't have to do any more of this brain-work. 'I KNEW that my Clever and

Intelligent Plan would work. And now I don't have to come up with another one! Watch and learn, my boy, watch and learn. It'll be a Fish Feast for supper then, guys!'

And off the Hooligan Warriors set, thinner and tireder and a great deal stinkier than normal, but as happy as anything at the thought of a limpet-free Fish Feast.

'And now, Toothless,' said Hiccup, in his sternest voice, 'hopefully my father will be in a better mood when he's got some food inside him, but still, you and I are going to tidy up what's left of that house before my father gets back.'

Toothless thought for a second. He put his head on one side.

'Weeeeelll,' said Toothless in the voice of a martyr. 'This wasn't T-t-toothless's fault... None of this is Toothless's fault... Was all those dragon babies...'

'Toothless!' interrupted Hiccup in exasperation. 'This was all your fault

entirely from start to finish! If you hadn't
stolen those Dreader eggs, the Dreader
wouldn't have followed us, and nobody
would have been hungry and—'

Toothless ignored him in a lofty way.
'And T-t-toothless is tired... Got a tummy
ache... W-w-want to go fishing...'

'I don't believe this,' said Hiccup.

'B-b-but...' said Toothless,
considering the matter, 'Toothless is not
a bad dragon like those dragon babies.
Toothless a GOOD, kind dragon, helpful,
thoughtful. Toothless sh-sh-shall help
the Mean Master – this time...' he
said kindly. 'Until Toothless's wings
start hurting.'

~ DRAGON BEHAVIOUR CHART ~

NAME: Toothless

BLACK MARK: X
STAR: ☆

	NO POOING	NO CHEWING	NO BURNING	NO STEALING	NO LYING
MONDAY	x X	x x	x x x	x x	x
TUESDAY	X	x x x	x x	x x	x
WEDNESDAY	X	x x x x	x x	x x	x
THURSDAY	x X	x x	x x	x x	x x
FRIDAY	X	x x x	x	x x	x
SATURDAY	x x X	x x x	x x	x x	x
SUNDAY	x	x x		x x	x

EPILOGUE

Well, Toothless DID help Hiccup clear up
that time (if you call 'helping' flying around
looking busy and tripping up Hiccup three
times by accident), and he tried to be good
for at least two weeks after that, before he
forgot what it was like to look after dragon
babies.

There was the most magnificent Fish
Feast in the Harbour that evening. Nobody
even bothered to go home first. They just
dumped the fish they'd caught on the rocks
and built a fire right then and there and ate
and ate until they were as full as fat
walruses.

And then, oh what dancing and
celebrating there was under the stars that
night!

Stoick was in such a good mood that
he barely even noticed the remains of the
destruction when he returned to the house.
Even he, however, could not fail to notice

the next morning the half-burned table, and the remains of the door. But Hiccup said it was a passing Tigerbreath who had done it, and Stoick was so smug with pride and full of belly that he believed him.

As for the stinkiness, well I'm afraid such was the stench of the Dreader-juices, the entire Isle of Berk reeked like dead haddock for at least a month or so afterwards.

But even that had its upside. The Uglithugs came creeping across in the dead of night on a deer-rustling raid on at least two occasions... and had to turn back when they came too close, on account of some of their younger Warriors feeling thoroughly ill at the pong.

Stoick never ate limpets again, and he never forgot his Clever and Intelligent Plan.

He had Fishlegs write him a small Saga called 'The Day of the Dreader', which exaggerated everything terribly.

Fishlegs called the Saga: 'The True

Story of What Really Happened on the Day of the Dreader.'

Fishlegs gave the Dreader every single terrible power he could think of. He added at least another foot to Stoick and gave him a long curling moustache as well. According to the Saga, Stoick not only had the brilliant Shield-Bashing Plan, he also fought the Dreader in hand-to-hand combat, and circled the Isle of Berk twice while holding on to one of the Dreader's tail fins.

So here we are at the beginning again.

Stories do not always tell the truth.

The bard gets carried away, legends get added to and exaggerated, and so gradually, gradually… the truth gets lost along the way…

Stories do not always tell the truth.

Except, of course, for this one.

HOW TO TRAIN YOUR DRAGON

Collect the whole series...

1: 978 0 340 99907 3

2: 978 0 340 99906 0

3: 978 0 340 99909 7

4: 978 0 340 99910 3

5: 978 0 340 99911 0

6: 978 0 340 99913 4

7: 978 0 340 99912 7

8: 978 0 340 99692 8

9: 978 1 444 90094 1

For exclusive competitions, dragon facts,
bonus stories and all the news
text **HICCUP** to **60777** (UK only)

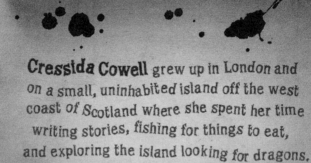

Cressida Cowell grew up in London and on a small, uninhabited island off the west coast of Scotland where she spent her time writing stories, fishing for things to eat, and exploring the island looking for dragons. She was convinced that there were dragons living on the island, and has been fascinated by them ever since.

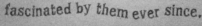

www.cressidacowell.co.uk

This is Cressida, age 9, writing on the island.

JOIN THE QUEST TO CREATE THE DEADLIEST DRAGON PROFILE

Create your own dragon profile by filling in
the template on the opposite page.

The deadliest dragons will be uploaded to
www.howtotrainyourdragonbooks.com
and the five best entries will be
selected to receive a set of signed
How to Train Your Dragon books.

Cut out and send your entry to:
How to Train Your Dragon World Book Day Competition
Hodder Children's Books, 338 Euston Road,
London, NW1 3BH

Don't forget to include your name and address!

Closing date: 27th April 2012

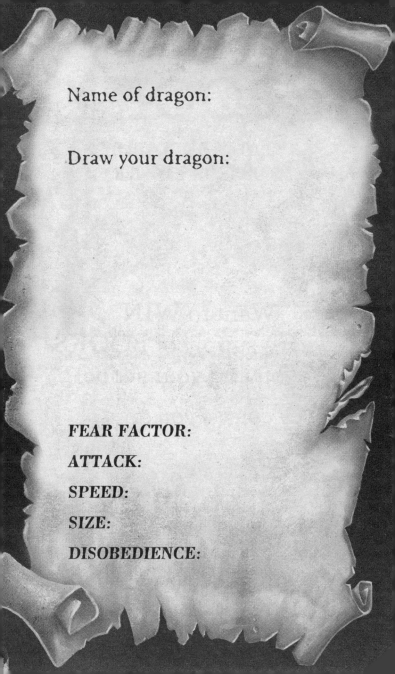

Name of dragon:

Draw your dragon:

FEAR FACTOR:

ATTACK:

SPEED:

SIZE:

DISOBEDIENCE:

WORLD
BOOK
DAY

1 MARCH 2012

Want to **WIN**
a year's supply of **BOOKS**
for you and your school?

Of course you do . . .

This book is by one of our favourite authors (that's why
it's in our **HALL OF FAME**!), but we want to know
what *your* favourite book is (or *your* favourite character
– whether it's the baddest baddie or the superest hero)!

It's that easy to win, so visit
WWW.WORLDBOOKDAY.COM now!